First published in paperback in Great Britain by HarperCollins Children's Books in 2007

3 5 7 9 10 8 6 4 2

ISBN-13: 978-0-00-718243-5

Text and illustrations copyright © Emma Chichester Clark 2007

HarperCollins Children's Books is a division of HarperCollins Publishers Ltd.
The author/illustrator asserts the moral right to be identified as the author/illustrator of the work.
A CIP catalogue record for this title is available from the British Library.

Visit our website at: www.harpercollins.co.uk

Printed in China

# Melrose and Croc

## GO TO TOWN

by Emma Chichester Clark

HarperCollins *Children's Books*

It was a lovely day.

"Let's go shopping!" said Little Green Croc.

"Okay," said Melrose, "but when we're in town
we must stick together and not get lost!"

"Come on!" said Little Green Croc.

"There's no rush," said Melrose.

"There's so much to do!" said Little Green Croc.

"We've got plenty of time," said Melrose.

"Come on!" cried Little Green Croc.

"Let's stick together!" said Melrose.

"Or else we'll get lost."

"Hurry up!" cried Little Green Croc.

"Look out!" said Melrose.

"Be careful!" said Melrose.

"Let's stick together, or else we'll get lost."

"This way!" cried Little Green Croc.

"Wait for me!" cried Melrose.

"WAIT!" cried Melrose.

"We must stick together, or else we'll get lost!"

"Oh no!" cried Melrose.

"Croc! Where are you?"

"Over here!" called Little Green Croc.

"Quick!" said Little Green Croc.

"Don't run!" said Melrose.

"Come back!" said Melrose.

"We've got to..."

"…stick together, or else we'll get lost."

"Where are you, Little Green Croc?" cried Melrose.

"Melrose! Where are you?"
cried Little Green Croc.

"Help!" cried Little Green Croc. "I'm lost!"

"There you are!" said Little Green Croc.

"There you are!" said Melrose.

"What shall we do next?" asked Melrose.
"Lets stick together, so we don't get lost,"
said Little Green Croc.

# Read all the stories about Melrose and Croc

**Melrose and Croc**
TOGETHER AT CHRISTMAS
by Emma Chichester Clark

Hardback ISBN: 978-0-00-719729-3
Paperback ISBN: 978-0-00-722593-4

It is Christmas Eve, and both Melrose and Croc are all alone in the city. They dream of a wonderful Christmas but feel sad for they have no one to share it with. And so it might have been were it not for the sound of beautiful music and a chance encounter. Could this be the beginning of a happy Christmas and even the start of a wonderful friendship?

ISBN: 978-0-00-718241-1

ISBN: 978-0-00-718242-8

*All £5.99*

ISBN: 978-0-00-718244-2

ISBN: 978-0-00-718243-5